ROCK-A-DOODLE-DO!

ORCHARD BOOKS

Why not visit
Shoo Rayner's website?
www.shoo-rayner.co.uk

ORCHARD BOOKS

96 Leonard Street, London EC2A 4XD

Orchard Books Australia

Unit 31/56 O'Riordan Street, Alexandria, NSW 2015

First published in Great Britain in 2000

First paperback edition 2001

Copyright © Shoo Rayner 2000

The right of Shoo Rayner to be identified as the
author and illustrator of this work has been asserted
by him in accordance with the
Copyright, Designs and Patents Act, 1988.

ISBN 1 84121 463 9 (hbk)

ISBN 1 84121 465 5 (pbk)

1 3 5 7 9 10 8 6 4 2 (hbk)

1 3 5 7 9 10 8 6 4 2 (pbk)

A CIP catalogue record for this book
is available from the British Library.

Printed in Great Britain

Down a quiet country lane,
through an arch of weeping
willow, an old Dutch barn sleeps
through the day.

But at six o'clock the lights
come on. The cars come rolling in.
Every night is party night at Old
MacDonald's drive-in.

Meet Wayne the manager.

Hey! Welcome to the coolest, tenpin bowling, rockin' and rolling, out of town farm-and-diner that any patch of starlit sky ever twinkled down upon.

Happy Hour 6-7
All the milk that you can drink!

Cindy used to be a waitress, here at Old MacDonald's drive-in. She had a dream, sweet as peaches and cream. She wanted to be a singing star.

Cindy's dad had played guitar in the famous Duke of Earl Band. Sometimes her mother sang in the band too. Singing was in Cindy's blood.

Late one night, Cindy was sweeping up when she found a crumpled poster.

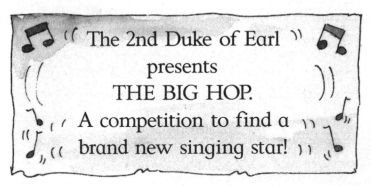

♪♪ "The 2nd Duke of Earl"
presents
THE BIG HOP.
A competition to find a
brand new singing star!

Her heart skipped a beat.

The second Duke of Earl! He's really famous...this could be my big chance!

But the poster stirred up memories
for Cindy too.

When she was just a little lamb,
the first Duke of Earl had flown his
band to California. But the plane
never landed, and the band,
including Cindy's mum and dad,
were never seen again.

Ever since, Cindy lived with her
Aunt Maybelline and her cousins,
Peggy and Sue.

Cindy felt a little sad. Quietly she
sang to herself. It was the song
her daddy used to sing to her.

Bye baby bunting,
Daddy's gone a-hunting,
Driving in his Chevrolet,
To buy some pretty dreams today.

Going down to Hollywood,
Santa Barbara too,
Ventura Highway,
Going my way,
Pacific Ocean blue.

You'll be safe,
You'll be warm,
Tucked up in L.A.
California dreaming,
In Daddy's Chevrolet.

To market, to market,
To buy a CD.
Doo-wop-she-diddy,
Play it for me.

Put it on quickly,
Play it out loud.
Doo-wop-she-diddy,
Play to the crowd.

Turn up the volume
To number eleven.
Doo-wop-she-diddy,
Hear it in heaven!

Seems to me,
the first thing you
need is a band.

You'll never believe what pulled up in the car park at that very same moment.

A chunka-lanking, second-rate ranking, beat up motorbus. With three crazy guys looking for gas, and maybe some bean stew and fresh rye bread. (If the late-night chef hadn't already gone to bed.)

Those Blue Diamond boys were as wild as a stormy night. They would play to anyone who'd listen.

They couldn't sing, though!

Boys! You've got style, you've got class, you've even got pazzazz. But you can't sing for peanuts. Let me show you someone who can really sing. Someone who is going to be a STAR!
La-la-la-dee-da!
sizzle
sizzle
sizzle
sizzle
She sure sings sweet, for a sheep!

There's lots of things we're not allowed, 🎵
'Cos Mum says, "Moany, moany".

We want to play our music loud, 🎵
But Mum says, "Moany, moany".

We'd beat the dustbins into drums, 🎵
But Mum says, "Moany, moany".

We've got guitars that we could strum, 🎵
But Mum says, "Moany, moany".

We'd sing our heads off, if we could, 🎵
But Mum says, "Moany, moany".

We need a place, where we can play, 🎵
on our owny, owny.

He found a crooked sixpence,
He found a crooked pound,
He bought a crooked radio,
With a crooked sound.

He yawned a crooked yawn,
And crookedly he said,
"I'm off to have a crooked sleep,
In my crooked bed!"

So he went to bed. He bumped his head, and never got up in the morning. He's been up those stairs ever since, listening to rock and roll on his crooked little radio.

He'd love to have a sha-la here, and a la-la there. Here a boop, there a shoop, everywhere a whoop-whoop! Yup! Old MacDonald's drive-in is where you're going to play.

So it was settled.

You are all going to the hop. You are going to practise till you drop. Let's start now. Get off your feet. Make it hot! Make it cool! Get working on that beat!

Drum-drum-drum,
With your thumb, thumb, thumb.

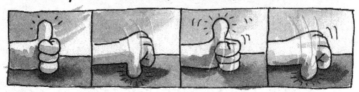

Rat-tat-tat,
With your fingers, just like that.

Boom-banga-boom,
With your feet,
And the words go...

Drum-drum-drum,
With your thumb,
Thumb, thumb...

Cindy and the band practised
all week long, trying different
sounds and styles.

Jazz,
Soul,
Rock and roll,
Bebop,
Jive and Swing,

Pop,
Trance,
Reggae...dance!
Get down,
And do your thing!

By Friday, the place was humming.
Cindy and the band played. The fans
kept coming.

Peggy and Sue dropped by with
Aunt Maybelline. She'd brought a
good luck gift for Cindy.

Cindy's cousins, Peggy and Sue, asked if they could sing some harmonies. After all, they'd been singing with Cindy for years.

Everyone had a turn at doing their own thing.

Let me play you my guitar,
Dinky-donky, dinky-donky.
One day I will be a star,
Dinky-donky, dinky-doo!

Let me play piano to you,
Plinky-plonky, plinky-plonky.
Do you like it? Tell me, do,
Plinky-plonky, plinky-poo!

Peggy and Sue were so good,
they became the Blue Diamond
backing singers.

The next day dawned
bright and fair.

The Blue Diamond Band climbed
aboard their bus, and set out on
the road to fame and fortune.

Everyone was nervous. They sang
to keep their spirits up.

Rock-a-bye baby,
Shang-a-lang-lye.
Rock-a-bye baby,
Don't you cry!

Rock-a-bye baby,
Rock-a-bye, hey!
We shall have music
All through the day.

Rock-a-bye baby
Shang-a-lang-lee.
We shall go dancing
Just you and me.

Rock-a-bye baby,
Shoo-wop-shee-doo.
We shall be dancing
Till quarter past two!

Blue Diamond Band

Welcome to the HOP!

The stage was in the middle of a field. The crowd sat all around. There were thousands in the audience, all waiting for the show to start.

The stage lit up. There stood Jack, the second Duke of Earl. The jewels on his coat twinkled in the spotlights.

To get you
in the mood,
I'd like to sing
you a song about
my old dad.

The Duke, Duke, Duke,
Duke of Earl, Earl, Earl,
Had a boy, boy, boy,
And a girl, girl, girl.

The boy was Jack, Jack, Jack,
The girl was Jill, Jill, Jill,
He marched them up, up, up,
Up the hill, hill, hill.

At the top, top, top,
Jack fell down, down, down,
All the way, way, way,
And broke his crown, crown, crown.

Jill fell too, too, too,
On her head, head, head,
So Jack and Jill, Jill, Jill,
Were sent to bed, bed, bed.

The Duke of Earl, Earl, Earl,
Was very sad, sad, sad,
He said I am, am, am,
A naughty dad, dad, dad.

He wrote it down, down, down,
With his pen, pen, pen,
We'll not go up, up, up,
That hill again.

The first act on stage were The Ten
Cool Cats. They were good.

Ten cool dudes,
Walking on the wall.
One tripped up,
He's heading for a fall.

Nine cool dudes,
Just hanging loose.
One got thirsty,
Drank some orange juice.

Eight cool dudes,
Dancing at the hop.
The hottest dude of all
Is the first one to stop.

Seven cool dudes,
Checking out their hair.
One had a wig on,
Which wasn't really fair.

Ouch!

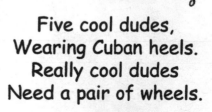

Six cool dudes,
Walking down the strip.
One got his hairy chest
Caught in his zip!

Five cool dudes,
Wearing Cuban heels.
Really cool dudes
Need a pair of wheels.

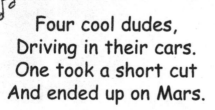

Errk!

Four cool dudes,
Driving in their cars.
One took a short cut
And ended up on Mars.

Three cool dudes,
Pumping iron on the beach.
Two were doing pull-ups,
One couldn't reach.

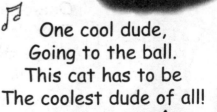

Two cool dudes,
Looking at each other.
One of them had to pay
A visit to his mother.

One cool dude,
Going to the ball.
This cat has to be
The coolest dude of all!

They were very good.
The audience loved them!
They got six lights on the Star Meter.

Jack got up and introduced the next act.

Come along now. Make some noise! Put your hands together for The Teddy Boys!

Round and round
The rockery,
Like a Teddy Boy,
One o'clock,
Two o'clock,
We all shout,
"Oi!"

That really got them going.
All that clapping pushed the
scoreboard up to seven.

Next came the mellow
sound of Little Boy Blue.

Little Boy Blue come blow your horn,
The rhythm has died,
The band are forlorn,
The dancers are sitting,
They're not on their feet,
Little Boy Blue, come, give us that beat.

Little Boy Blue come blow your horn,
The melody's faded,
The lyrics are worn,
The song it is dying,
It's barely alive,
Little Boy Blue, come, gimme some jive.

Would the applause ever stop?
Eight lights were on the Star
Meter as Cindy and the Blue
Diamond Band took the stage.
Could they beat that score?

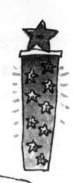

Little Boy Blue
got me right there
in the heart. Now,
Cindy and the Blue
Diamond Band are
ready to start!

Mmmm...
He's got me
right there in the
heart, too!

As they began to play, midnight chimed on a distant church bell.

Doing! Doing! Doing!

Little Bo-peep
Has lost her sheep.
Ba-ba-Barbara-Anne
She's got so worried,
She just can't sleep.
Ba-ba-Barbara-Anne

The sheep got together
In a mighty big flock.
Ba-ba-Barbara-Anne
It's the middle of the night,
And the sheep are gonna rock.

Ba-ba-Barbara-Anne!

She is just gor-jee-us!

They danced the twist,
They danced the stroll.
Ba-ba-Barbara-Anne
They wiggled their hips,
They shook their wool.
Ba-ba-Barbara-Anne

Time to go home,
Yackety-yak.
Ba-ba-Barbara-Anne
Wagging their tails
All the way back.
Ba-ba-Barbara-Anne

Little Bo-peep
Has found her sheep.
Ba-ba-Barbara-Anne
All the little lambs
Are fast asleep.
Ba-ba-Barbara-Anne

The crowd went wild. They stormed the stage. It was a free-for-all, a farmyard rampage!

Ten bright lights dazzled on the scoreboard. But Cindy had disappeared, leaving a single shoe upon the stage.

Jack gently picked it up. His heart
was well and truly smit! He'd found
the girl that he was looking for!

The band played. Cindy and Jack
fell into each other's arms and
danced the night away!

Rock-a-doodle-do!
The dame has lost her shoe.
On midnight's strike
She screamed, "Oh yikes!
There's something I must do."

Rock-a-doodle-do!
What is the Duke to do?
He could dance all night
With his heart's delight,
But he hasn't said how do you do!

Rock-a-doodle-do!
The Duke has found her shoe.
"Whoever this fits
I'll kiss to bits,
And I promise I'll marry her too!"

Rock-a-doodle-do!
The dame, she fits the shoe.
"Now, my dame,
Won't you tell me your name?
Then I can say how do you do?"

Rock-a-doodle-do!
The dame has got her shoe.
So Cindy can tell her
Brand new feller,
That she'd only gone to the loo!

The End